In the night, i pulled my hometown in and nestled it on my lap

晚上　我把故鄉拉了進來

放在我大腿上

Bird droppings on the eaves

空的屋簷上有鳥糞

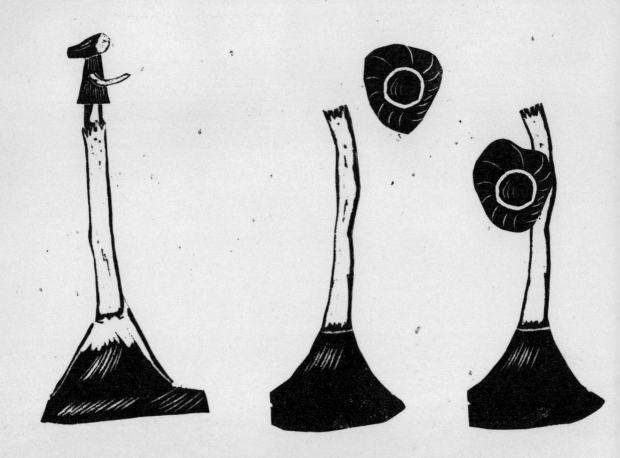

Gecko on the empty wall

空的牆壁上有壁虎

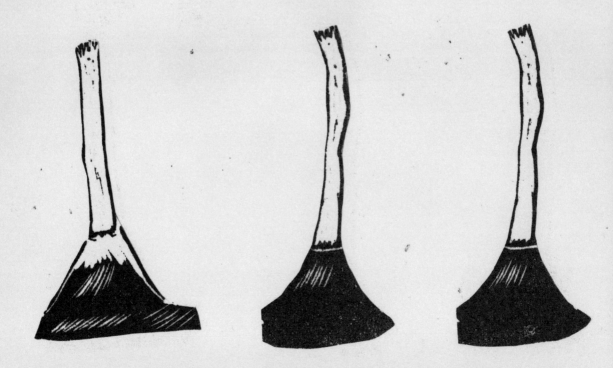

Frogs sing loudly outside

Sang for three hundred and sixty-five days

外面有青蛙大聲唱

唱了三百六十五天

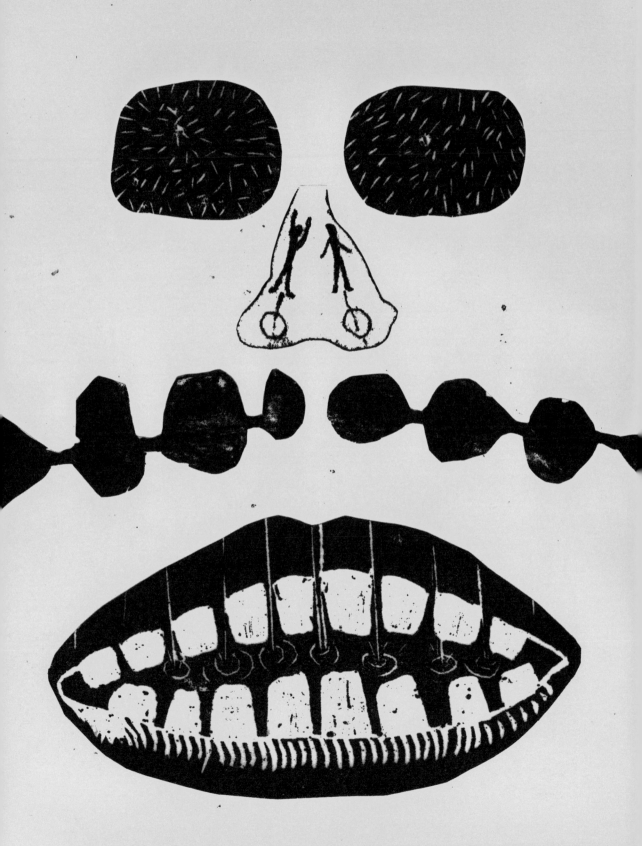

The weeds tell the stray cat

The mangoes are ripe

野草和野貓說

芒果成熟了

The fallen leaves pile on the ground

落了滿地厚厚的葉

落葉下有一條通道

The fallen leaves creates a path

A path to the mosquito's home

通去蚊子的家

Flying from here to there

The mosquito asks a spider

Can you write poems

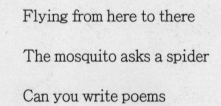

從這裏飛去那裏

蚊子問蜘蛛

你會寫詩嗎

On an empty chair

在一張空的椅子上

On an empty bed

在一張空的床上

I wrote the poem

我把詩寫好了

馬尼尼為 maniniwei

馬來西亞華人，苟生台北逾二十年。美術系所出身卻反感美術系，三十歲後重拾創作。作品包括散文、詩、繪本。《帶著你的雜質發亮》、《我不是生來當母親的》、《我們明天再說話》、《馬惹尼》、《詩人旅館》、《老人臉狗書店》等十餘冊。曾任臺北詩歌節主視覺設計，作品入選台灣年度詩選、散文選，獲國藝會文學與視覺藝術補助數次。於博客來 OKAPI、小典藏撰寫讀書筆記和繪本專欄。2020 獲 OPENBOOK 好書獎：年度中文創作；桃園市立美術館展出和駐館藝術家。2021 獲選香港浸會大學華語駐校作家、鍾肇政文學獎散文正獎、金鼎獎文學圖書獎。

A Malaysian Chinese, stay at Taiwan for 20 years with two or three cats and one child. Published over ten books included prose, poetry, picture books and a Malay Pantun illustrated book and 100 Malay Ghost. 2020 OPENBOOK best literature book award, 2021 Hong Kong Baptist University writer in residence, 2021 Golden Tripod Awards Taiwan.

Fb/ IG / website keyword : maniniwei

國家圖書館出版品預行編目（CIP）資料

姐姐的空房子 / 馬尼尼為文、圖 . -- 初版 . --
新北市：斑馬線出版社，2021.12
面； 公分
中英對照
ISBN 978-626-95412-0-1（平裝）

859.8   110020167

姐姐的空房子

文、圖：馬尼尼為
策劃、出版：馬尼尼為
英譯：Ng Jia Xuan
發行：斑馬線文庫有限公司
My sister's empty house
©2021 Maniniwei
https://maniniwei.wixsite.com/maniniwei
First Edition
Printed in Taiwan

斑馬線文庫
通訊地址：234 新北市永和區民光街 20 巷 7 號 1 樓
連絡電話：0922542983

製版印刷：龍虎電腦排版股份有限公司
出版日期：2021 年 12 月
ISBN：978-626-95412-0-1
定　　價：380 元